THE MENTOR'S CHALK

A Story from The Old is Forever New Series

GREGORY REICHMUTH

Copyright Page
Mastering the Classroom, LLC®: The Old is Forever New Series®
Volume 1: The Mentor's Chalk
Copyright © 2024 by Gregory Reichmuth

Published by Gregory Reichmuth
2910 Magnolia Street, Denver, CO. 80207
ISBN 978-1-965957-00-4 Digital
ISBN 978-1-965957-02-8 EPUB
ISBN 978-1-965957-01-1 Paperback
Library of Congress Control Number:
1-14356190491

This is a work of historical fiction. While some historical events, locations, and characters are based on factual sources, others have been created or altered for narrative purposes. The information within is a blend of history and fiction and is intended to provide insight into the subject matter covered, with no claim of historical accuracy for fictionalized portions.

Printed in the United States of America

Author Bio:
Gregory Reichmuth

Gregory Reichmuth is a passionate and dedicated educational leader with over 20 years of experience. He currently teaches in the Engineering & Programming Department at STEM School Highlands Ranch in Colorado and has previously served in Denver Public Schools, where he was recognized for his commitment to accountability and educational excellence while working in the Alternative Educational Program.

Dr. Rodney Blunck, Associate Clinical Professor at the University of Colorado Denver, describes Gregory as "one of the most passionate and accountability-oriented educational leaders" he has ever worked with. Known for his action-oriented leadership, Gregory consistently challenges the status quo and remains deeply committed to social justice and public education. He excels at fostering cohesion among staff, developing collective purpose, and advocating for students, families, and communities.

Gregory's leadership style is defined by integrity, clear communication, and a collaborative approach. He inspires others with his visionary energy and enthusiasm, always working to create a better educational environment. As Dr. Blunck notes, Gregory "models' leadership, sets clear goals and objectives, and holds high expectations for colleagues and staff."

In addition to his professional work, Gregory is the author of two notable book series. *The Old is Forever New Series* is a collection of historically rooted fictional stories that explore educational principles through the lens of past events, blending historical accuracy with powerful narratives. *The Discovery Series* addresses modern educational challenges, offering educators practical insights and strategies to create world-class learning environments that meet today's needs.

Dedication

To my beloved mother, Barbara Ann Reichmuth
(1941 - 2024).

Your unwavering love, wisdom, and inspiration have shaped the person I am today. Your strength, kindness, and dedication to our family and your endless encouragement to pursue my dreams will forever be remembered and cherished.

This book series is dedicated to you, Mom. Your spirit lives on in every word, and your legacy of inspiration continues to guide me. Thank you for being my guiding light and my greatest supporter. I love you and miss you every day.

**IN LOVING MEMORY,
GREGORY REICHMUTH**

Contents

Introduction

The Mentor's Chalk

In the bustling streets of 1850s New York City, Samuel, a dedicated teacher, faces the challenges of an evolving society while striving to shape the minds of his students. As new educational ideas emerge and social tensions rise, Samuel must navigate the complexities of his classroom, where each child's future is intertwined with the changing world around them.

The Mentor's Chalk is a powerful tale of mentorship, resilience, and the transformative power of education. The first story in The Old is Forever New Series®, it brings to life the struggles and triumphs of an era when the foundations of modern education were being built. Readers will be drawn into a world where the lessons learned in the classroom extend far beyond its walls.

Manuscript
The Mentor's Chalk
By Gregory Reichmuth
September 20, 2024

Time Period: 1853 Theme:

Mentorship, Early Education Reforms, Personal Growth Character Focus: Samuel (mentor), Abigail (protagonist)

Summary:

A young teacher named Abigail navigates the challenges of teaching during a time of great change in New York City. Guided by her mentor, Samuel, she learns that education is more than facts and figures— it's about shaping character and community.

CHAPTER 1

New York City, 1853

The bitter tang of coal smoke lingered in the damp morning air as Samuel leaned out of the small carriage window, taking in the sprawling chaos of New York City. Buildings rose like jagged teeth from the earth, their facades alternating between the grandeur of brownstone mansions and the peeling, soot-streaked walls of crowded tenements. Above, the sky hung low, its heavy gray clouds casting the streets below in a dull, oppressive light. Samuel's gaze flitted from one corner of the city to another, trying to make sense of the bustling metropolis that seemed to swell and heave like a living beast around him.

This was a city of contradictions—of wealth and poverty, of splendor and filth. It was also a city in the midst of transformation. Construction sites littered the streets, signs of a growing and modernizing city. He could see cranes in the distance, towering over incomplete structures like **St. Patrick's Cathedral**, and new brownstone mansions rising to house the city's wealthiest families. The sounds of hammering and the clatter of horse-drawn carts filled the air, blending with the ever-present hum of human activity.

As his carriage rattled over the cobblestones, past **Castle Garden** in Battery Park, the weight of his mission bore down on him. Crowds of immigrants milled about near the port, their faces lined with fatigue and hope. For many, this was their first glimpse of America—a land of opportunity yet fraught with its own struggles. Samuel marveled at the sheer magnitude of humanity surging into the city. The air was thick with the sounds of a dozen different languages—Irish, German, Italian—each one a story of survival and dreams for a better life. He couldn't help but think of how these new arrivals would soon shape New York's future, and perhaps, the students he would teach.

His thoughts drifted briefly to **Frederick Douglass**, whose words had inspired him during his years in training. Douglass had spoken of education as the "pathway from slavery to freedom," and Samuel had taken that to heart. Though the children he would be teaching were not enslaved, many of them faced lives filled with poverty and hardship. It was through education, Samuel believed, that they might find their way out. Douglass had often spoken of how literacy opened his eyes to the injustices of the world, and Samuel carried that ideal with him now.

The carriage jolted to a halt, and Samuel stepped out gingerly, his boots sinking into the thick mud near the curb. As he adjusted his coat, a sharp voice pierced through the noise of the city.

"New York Daily Times! Latest news on the Irish!"

A boy, no older than twelve, darted through the crowd with a bundle of newspapers under his arm. His face was smudged with dirt, his clothes worn thin, but his eyes gleamed with energy. "Get your paper here! More Irish comin' in every day!"

Samuel's attention was drawn to the boy, who skidded to a stop beside him, offering a newspaper. "You want the news, sir? They're comin' in by the boatloads. My pa says soon enough, this whole city'll be Irish!"

Samuel couldn't help but smile at the boy's boldness. "What's your name?"

"Liam, sir. Liam O'Connor," the boy replied, puffing out his chest with a mix of pride and youthful confidence.

Samuel fished a coin from his pocket and handed it to Liam, taking the newspaper. "Thank you, Liam. And your father's right—New York is growing, faster than anyone can imagine."

Liam grinned. "Aye, it is! More of us Irish comin' every day. You new here, sir?"

"I am," Samuel said, scanning the headlines. His eyes landed on a bold headline: **Southern Slavery; A Glance at Uncle Tom's Cabin**. The weight of the article struck him. Harriet Beecher Stowe's novel was stirring the nation—praised by abolitionists in the North, condemned by the South. The debate over slavery, Samuel knew, would not remain distant; it would soon become a conversation in his classroom.

Liam, seeing the shift in Samuel's expression, tilted his head. "That story's been causin' quite a stir. My pa says it's nonsense, but my ma… she says it makes people think."

Samuel nodded thoughtfully, folding the paper under his arm. "Sometimes, that's all it takes—something to make people think."

Liam gave a quick wave, already darting back into the bustling crowd, his voice calling out once more for customers. Samuel watched him disappear, his words blending into the city's constant hum.

CHAPTER 2

Journey Through the City

Samuel stepped onto the slick cobblestones, the dampness of the city clinging to him like a second skin. His boots slipped slightly on the uneven stones, slick from a recent rain that had left the streets glistening in the weak light. New York's pulse was unmistakable, an incessant hum of life that vibrated through the soles of his boots, rising up into his very bones. Every breath he took felt thick and labored, filled with the mingling scents of coal smoke, wet wood, and the sharp, metallic tang of factory exhaust. The city seemed to breathe with him, exhaling grit and industry, its air tasting of toil and exhaustion.

He moved through the crowd, his senses assaulted by the raw energy that surrounded him. Vendors lined the streets, their carts cluttered with oysters, steaming chestnuts, and jars of pickled vegetables. The sharp, sour tang of vinegar cut through the musty odor of the streets, mingling with the scent of sweat and smoke. Voices rose above the din, a blend of accents—Irish, Italian, German—each one sharp, insistent, competing for attention in the chaotic marketplace. He could see the grand silhouette of **Trinity Church** in the distance, standing like a beacon amidst the surrounding chaos.

Samuel weaved through the throng, the steady din of bartering and laughter forming a strange contrast to the faces of those who moved through the streets. They were drawn, tired, their expressions hardened by the daily grind of survival. Men with hunched shoulders and hollow eyes shuffled past him, their hands stained with the labor of the docks and factories. Their movements were slow, deliberate, as if every step required a calculation, a choice between conserving energy and making it home.

As he turned down a narrower street, the city seemed to change. The buildings leaned in toward each other, their facades darkened by years of soot and neglect, as if the very architecture was sagging under the weight of time and hardship. Windows stared down at him like hollow, vacant eyes, their glass cracked and clouded from decades of grime. Above, clotheslines hung between the buildings, sagging with the weight of damp laundry that swayed listlessly in the stagnant air, never quite drying in the relentless humidity that clung to the city.

The alleyways were a maze of shadows, filled with children who darted between the buildings, their bare feet slapping against the wet stones. Their laughter echoed briefly, sharp and bright, cutting through the grayness for only a moment before being swallowed again by the city's relentless hum. Their faces, smudged with dirt, bore the haunted look of children too young to have seen so much hardship. They played, but their play felt forced, as if childhood had become a fleeting thing, a brief interlude between moments of survival.

Above them, mothers leaned out of windows, their voices sharp with reprimands that cut through the noise below. Their eyes, lined with exhaustion, swept over the streets like hawks, watching their children but also watching the world that encroached on them, the world that pressed in on all sides, unyielding. Samuel caught their gazes as he passed, saw the hard lines of their faces—women who had learned long ago that softness was a luxury they could not afford.

The deeper he walked into the heart of the city, the heavier his own heart became. The poverty here wasn't just visible; it was a living thing, woven into the fabric of the city itself. It clung to the people like the soot on the bricks, weighing them down, stifling any breath of hope before it could truly take root. Samuel could feel it—an oppressive force that hung in the air, making every step feel like it required more effort than the last.

Samuel paused in front of **Tammany Hall**, the center of New York's political machine. Its imposing brick structure loomed above him, a symbol of the power and corruption that ruled the city. He had read about the political struggles in the papers, how men like **Frederick Douglass** and other abolitionists tried to use education and rhetoric to counterbalance the weight of entrenched power. But here, standing on the bustling street, those efforts seemed small against the backdrop of New York's immensity.

Still, Samuel knew that education was the only weapon he had to make a difference. He moved on, determined to find his way to the school, to begin the work that lay ahead of him.

CHAPTER 3

Arrival at the School

When Samuel finally reached the schoolhouse, he stood still, his breath catching in his throat. Before him, the building seemed to sag beneath the weight of its years, its once-bright wood siding now dulled to a peeling, splintered gray, like a relic too long exposed to the unforgiving elements. Time had gnawed at it, stripping away whatever pride or promise it might have once held. The windows, opaque with grime, reflected only the ghost of the city—a weary, exhausted version of what stood beyond the walls. Above the door, a crooked sign swung lazily in the breeze, held aloft by a single, rusted nail. The bold, cracked lettering proclaimed its name with an irony too bitter to ignore: *School for the City's Youth*. It was a title that seemed almost mocking, too grand for the huddled structure it marked, too hopeful for a place so burdened by neglect.

Samuel's chest tightened. He inhaled deeply, but the air offered little relief. It was thick and damp, laced with the musty scent of decay, mingling with the sharp tang of wood smoke and something sour that he couldn't quite place. The faint aroma of burning wood hung in the air as he approached the door, a reminder that this schoolhouse—like the students it sheltered—was scraping by on the barest of essentials. As he reached out, the rough, weathered wood of the door seemed to resist his touch, groaning in protest as he pushed it open.

The hallway greeted him with a blast of thick, stifling heat that felt almost oppressive. A cast-iron stove stood at the far end of the corridor, its surface blackened by years of soot and use. The stove radiated warmth, but not the comforting kind—it was the kind that suffocated rather than soothed, clashing with the cool dampness that clung to the walls and the faint chill that lingered in the air. Samuel could feel the uneven floorboards shift slightly beneath his feet as he stepped inside, each creak of the wood echoing loudly in the otherwise stifling silence. The place felt as though it was waiting, holding its breath, as if even the building had learned to expect little from the world.

Dust floated lazily in the weak shafts of light filtering through the grimy windows, drifting down to settle on the cracked plaster walls, which bore the scars of long-forgotten attempts at repair. He moved slowly down the narrow hallway, his fingers brushing lightly against the rough wooden banisters that had long since lost their polish. Each step felt deliberate, cautious, as if the entire building might crumble beneath the weight of his presence. The silence pressed in on him, broken only by the distant crackling of the wood in the stove's belly, the sound as fragile as the place itself.

As Samuel passed by the open doorways of classrooms, he glanced inside. Rows of desks sat in silent formation, warped and uneven, their surfaces scarred by years of use. The wood was etched with the markings of students long gone—initials carved in haste, faded names, the occasional crude drawing. There was something profoundly sad about it, as if the desks themselves bore witness to generations of children who had come and gone, each leaving behind only the faintest trace of their presence. The smell of wet wood and ash hung heavy in the air, mingling with the faint, acrid scent of something burnt—perhaps a remnant of the stove's relentless labor.

The schoolhouse felt ancient, like a relic from another time, held together not by sturdy construction but by sheer necessity. Every corner seemed to sag under the weight of neglect, every surface worn thin by years of hard use and too little care. And yet, there was something else here too, something just beneath the surface—a sense of potential, of hope buried beneath the layers of grime and disrepair. It was faint, almost imperceptible, but Samuel could feel it. The children who walked through these doors each day, those whose laughter had faded into the wood and whose dreams had scratched the desks, deserved more than this place had to offer. They deserved a chance.

Samuel stood still for a moment, letting the silence wash over him. The enormity of the task ahead weighed on him, heavier than he had expected. But the building, for all its decay and wear, was still standing. So, too, were the children who came here, day after day, hoping for something better. And Samuel, no matter how overwhelming it felt, was determined to give them that chance.

CHAPTER 4

At the Boarding House

By the time Samuel reached the boarding house, the sun had dipped low behind the jagged skyline, casting long shadows over the narrow streets. The evening air was thick with the lingering scent of coal smoke and damp earth, and the city had settled into a quieter rhythm. As Samuel passed by **The Hotel Saint Nicholas**, its grand facade stood as a testament to New York's growing wealth and luxury. Opened in 1853, the hotel catered to the city's elite, its towering presence and opulent decor a stark contrast to the more humble accommodations scattered across the city. The gleaming windows reflected the soft glow of gas lamps, and as Samuel walked by, he could see the well-dressed guests moving about inside—people whose lives were worlds away from the struggles of the students he would soon teach.

His destination, however, was far from the grandeur of the Saint Nicholas. **O'Brien's Boarding House**—a modest brick building nestled between two larger structures—seemed almost hidden in the fading light. Ivy crept up its facade, softening the weathered edges of the bricks, and a small wooden sign swung lazily in the breeze above the door, the words "O'Brien's Boarding House" barely visible through years of wear.

Samuel paused at the doorstep, adjusting his grip on the small bag that held his belongings. Despite its unremarkable appearance, the building exuded a quiet charm, offering a sense of respite after the relentless bustle of the city. He pushed open the door, which groaned under his touch, and stepped inside. The scent of old wood, faint tobacco, and something sweet—lavender, perhaps—greeted him, wrapping him in a familiar warmth. The narrow hallway was dimly lit by a single lamp, casting a soft glow over the faded wallpaper that lined the walls, its once vibrant floral pattern now barely discernible.

Mrs. O'Brien, the landlady, bustled out from the back of the house, her presence filling the small space with lively energy. A stout woman with rosy cheeks and a neat bun, her apron dusted with flour, she wiped her hands briskly as she approached. The aroma of freshly baked bread wafted from the kitchen behind her, a comforting contrast to the sharp city air Samuel had just left behind.

"Ah, you must be the new teacher!" she exclaimed, her thick Irish accent carrying the warmth of someone well-practiced in hospitality. "Come in, come in! You're a bit early for supper, but I'll show you to your room first."

Samuel nodded gratefully, appreciating the warm reception. Mrs. O'Brien led him up a creaky wooden staircase, each step groaning beneath their weight. The hallway upstairs was lined with doors, their dark wood worn smooth from years of use. Behind each one, Samuel imagined the lives of the other boarders unfolding—quiet conversations, the rustling of clothes, the scraping of chairs as people settled in for the evening.

"You'll be in here," Mrs. O'Brien said, opening the door to a small room at the end of the hall. The room was simple, but cozy. A narrow bed, neatly made with a thick woolen blanket, sat beneath a small window that overlooked the quiet street below. A wooden dresser with a cracked mirror stood against the wall, and the faint scent of lavender—no doubt from sachets placed carefully beneath the bed—hung in the air, lending the room a surprising touch of comfort.

"It's simple, but it's clean," Mrs. O'Brien said with a nod of satisfaction. "The others will be down for supper soon—Mr. Donnelly works at the docks, Miss Perkins is a seamstress, and Mr. Hargrove, well, he's a teacher like yourself. All good folk. You'll fit in just fine."

Samuel smiled, the tension of the day finally beginning to ease. "Thank you, Mrs. O'Brien. This will do perfectly."

After she left, the room grew still, save for the faint sounds of the city beyond the window. Samuel sat on the edge of the bed, letting the weight of the day settle on him like the woolen blanket at his side. He glanced at the few belongings he had brought with him—his books, a change of clothes, and the **New York Daily Times** he had bought from the paperboy, Liam, earlier that day. The headline from the article still weighed heavily on his mind: **Southern Slavery; A Glance at Uncle Tom's Cabin.**

As he unfolded the newspaper and began to read, Samuel's thoughts wandered to the students he would soon meet, wondering how they would receive him, and how they would respond to the difficult lessons that lay ahead. The challenges seemed monumental, but for now, in this quiet, modest room, he allowed himself a moment of calm. Tomorrow, the real work would begin.

CHAPTER 5

The First Day of School

The morning light filtered weakly through the grime-coated windows of the schoolhouse, casting thin, pale rays across the room, barely illuminating the dust that hung in the air. The faint shafts of sunlight seemed almost reluctant to enter, as if even the light itself was hesitant to disturb the silence. Samuel stood before the cracked chalkboard, his fingers gripping a piece of chalk so tightly that his knuckles whitened. His hand trembled ever so slightly, a visible manifestation of the nervous energy swirling inside him.

The room was eerily quiet, the kind of silence that carries weight, thick and expectant. Every eye in the room was fixed on him, waiting, measuring. Samuel could feel their collective gaze like a physical force, the unspoken expectations pressing down on him, mingling with the rising tension in his chest. He had prepared for this moment, but nothing in his training could have prepared him for the way his heart pounded now, for the way the air itself seemed charged with the potential for failure or triumph.

For a moment, his hand hovered just above the chalkboard, the chalk poised in midair. He hesitated, feeling the enormity of what he was about to write—not just a word, but an idea, a concept that had the power to ignite something in these students or, just as easily, fall flat. His thoughts raced as he imagined the lives of the children sitting before him, shaped by hardship, by the city's grit and unrelenting demands. Did the word *freedom* mean anything in a place where survival itself was a daily struggle?

With deliberate care, he pressed the chalk to the board, and in slow, sweeping motions, he scrawled the word: *freedom*. The chalk screeched faintly against the worn surface, the sound cutting through the silence like a knife. The letters were uneven, but bold, standing stark against the weathered blackboard. Samuel stepped back, eyeing the word as if it might hold the answers to the questions that loomed larger than this classroom, larger than the city outside.

He turned slowly to face his students. Their faces were a mixture of curiosity, skepticism, and the quiet defiance of youth. Some leaned forward slightly, their attention caught by the word on the board, while others remained still, their expressions unreadable. Samuel's heart thudded in his chest as he searched their faces, wondering what they saw in him—an outsider, a man with ideals that might not fit in a world so hardened by necessity.

His gaze first landed on Maria, seated by the window. The sunlight played across her face, casting soft shadows that made her look older than her years. Her hands were clasped tightly in her lap, her knuckles pale, as though she were holding onto something invisible but heavy. Her eyes, however, were cast downward, lost in some inner world, far removed from the classroom and the word scrawled on the chalkboard. Samuel wondered what burdens Maria carried, what silent battles she fought within herself that made her retreat from the idea of freedom.

In contrast, Liam sat near the front, his posture practically leaning forward with eagerness. His eyes were bright, brimming with thoughts and opinions he seemed barely able to contain. Samuel could almost feel the boy's energy radiating outward, as if Liam was ready to burst into debate at the slightest provocation. There was a fire in him, a hunger for something beyond the narrow confines of the world he had known. Liam's passion was unmistakable, and it was clear that for him, *freedom* wasn't just a word—it was a promise, something to be grasped and claimed.

At the back of the room sat Hans, his arms crossed tightly over his chest, his posture rigid with defiance. His eyes were narrowed, watching Samuel with a look that hovered somewhere between suspicion and challenge. There was tension in the way he held himself, an almost palpable resistance. Hans didn't need to speak for Samuel to know that this was a boy who had already decided what he thought of the world, and it wasn't going to change easily. Freedom, for Hans, was likely an abstraction, something others talked about but which had little bearing on the practical realities of life. He was waiting for Samuel to justify himself, to say something worth listening to.

Samuel swallowed, feeling the dryness in his throat tighten as the weight of the room pressed down on him. His eyes flicked briefly to his desk, where the folded newspaper lay—its headline about *Uncle Tom's Cabin* still fresh in his mind. That headline whispered to him, a reminder that today wasn't just about teaching the usual subjects. Today was about something deeper. Something that stretched far beyond the cracked walls of this worn-out classroom.

Clearing his throat, Samuel straightened his shoulders. He could feel the anticipation in the room, the students waiting for him to make the first move. He couldn't fail them, not now.

"Today," he began, his voice steady but his heart racing, "we're going to talk about what freedom really means."

The word *freedom* hung in the air like a question yet to be answered, its weight pressing down on everyone in the room. A few students shifted in their seats, the tension palpable as they waited to see where this would go. The pale light from the windows flickered across the cracked walls, as if even the building itself was holding its breath.

"This isn't just about what we read in books," Samuel continued, his eyes moving from one student to the next, making sure to meet each of their gazes, even Hans's, whose eyes still bore the stubborn glare of defiance. "It's about how we live, how we think, and how we act in the world. Freedom is not just something we are given. It's something we must define for ourselves."

Liam's head bobbed up and down in vigorous agreement, his hands gripping the edge of his desk as though he could barely contain his excitement. Samuel could almost see the thoughts swirling behind the boy's eyes, the eager passion for debate already stirring in him. Liam was the kind of student who would throw himself into any discussion, ready to fight for his beliefs, no matter the odds.

But Maria remained still, her fingers still twisted together in her lap, as though the weight of the word *freedom* was too much for her to bear. She shrank inward, as though retreating from the very idea of it, as if it held questions she wasn't ready to face, answers she couldn't yet give voice to.

In the back, Hans shifted in his seat, his expression hardening. His eyes narrowed, as though he were dissecting the very concept of freedom, already deciding whether it was worth his attention. Samuel knew Hans would be the challenge. For a boy like Hans, freedom was something abstract, shaped by his family's rigid views, their wealth, and their position. It wasn't a concept that aligned easily with the rules he had been taught to live by.

Taking a step forward, Samuel gestured toward the chalkboard. "So, what do you think it means?" he asked, his voice soft but deliberate. "What does freedom look like in your life?"

The room remained silent for a moment longer, the tension thick and unyielding as Samuel waited for someone—anyone—to break the stillness. Finally, as expected, Liam's hand shot into the air, his voice eager and sure.

"Freedom means not being told what to do!" he exclaimed, the words tumbling out of him in a rush. "It means choosing your own path, not letting someone else decide it for you."

Samuel nodded, but before he could respond, Hans's voice cut through the room, low and grumbling. "That's easy to say," Hans muttered, his arms tightening across his chest. "But we all have rules we need to follow. Without them, everything falls apart."

Samuel watched the interplay between the two boys, the passion in Liam's voice clashing with the cool pragmatism of Hans's words. The divide was clear, and yet both perspectives carried weight. The debate wasn't just about the concept of freedom—it was about how each of these students saw their world, shaped by their own experiences and the expectations they carried.

Maria's eyes flickered up for just a moment, and Samuel caught the briefest glimpse of something in her gaze—a conflict, perhaps, or a question left unspoken. She understood, more than anyone, the complexity of the word *freedom*, but she wasn't ready to voice it. Not yet.

The room was poised on the edge of something—Samuel could feel it. The lesson had begun, but it was far from over.

CHAPTER 6

Maria's Background

Maria had grown up in a household where even the walls seemed to listen, where conversations about justice were whispered, carried on in hushed tones, as though any word too loud might unravel everything. The dim kitchen was the heart of these whispered exchanges—her father's voice low and steady, her mother's fingers twisting in anxious circles around the hem of her apron. The aroma of freshly brewed coffee mingled with the damp scent of rain-soaked earth, the soft patter against the windowpane a constant reminder that even in their home, safety was never guaranteed. Every moment felt fragile, like the air itself could betray them.

One night in particular lingered in Maria's memory. She had been no older than nine, tucked under her quilt, the fabric pulled tightly to her chin. Sleep had eluded her, her heart racing as the muffled voices of her parents drifted through the paper-thin walls. The urgency in their tones was unmistakable. She strained to listen, catching fragments of the conversation—a family friend, a runaway slave hidden in their home, the law closing in like a tightening noose.

Her father's voice, usually calm and measured, was clipped with a fear Maria had never heard before. It wasn't just the law they feared, he had said. It was the neighbors—their community. Whispers traveled faster than truth in their tight-knit town, and suspicion spread like wildfire. Maria lay awake long after her parents had fallen silent, staring at the ceiling, her young mind conjuring shadows that stretched and twisted across the walls, their shapes as haunting as the danger that seemed to close in on her family.

Her father's words from that night had never left her. *Doing what's right isn't about being brave—it's about feeling afraid and acting anyway.* Those words had settled deep into Maria's heart, a steady current beneath her thoughts as she grew older. She had watched her father's hands tremble when he spoke of the risks they took, had seen the furrows in her mother's brow grow deeper with each passing day. And yet, they stood firm in their beliefs. Right was right, no matter the cost. Even if the cost was fear.

Now, as Maria sat in Samuel's classroom, that same fear twisted in her gut, a familiar knot that tightened with each passing moment. The sunlight filtered weakly through the dirt-smeared windows, casting pale shadows across the cracked walls. But the warmth of the light did little to dispel the chill that settled deep in her bones. She shifted in her seat, her hands clasped tightly in her lap, her fingers digging into the worn fabric of her dress. The word *freedom* loomed on the chalkboard, but Maria's mind was far from the lesson at hand.

Sarah. That was where her thoughts drifted—to the narrow, dark cellar beneath her home, where Sarah, a runaway slave, huddled in hiding. Maria had brought her food, whispered soft words of comfort into the shadows, but with every visit, the weight on her chest seemed to grow heavier. Each time Maria closed the cellar door behind her, she felt like she was leaving part of herself in that damp, suffocating space. She had taken

Sarah in, but the fear that accompanied that act of kindness never left her. It hung over her like a storm cloud, threatening to break at any moment.

Every step she took on the way to school felt like balancing on a razor's edge, as if one wrong move, one wrong word, could send everything tumbling down. What if someone found out? What would happen to her family, to Sarah? The questions haunted her, their sharp edges cutting through her every thought, cold and relentless. The weight of responsibility pressed down on her like a hand around her throat, tight and unyielding.

Her father's voice echoed in her mind: *It's not about feeling brave. It's about feeling scared and doing what's right anyway.* But fear was a constant companion now, wrapping itself around her home, her family, and every quiet, stolen interaction with Sarah. Maria could see it in the way her mother's eyes flickered toward the windows, checking for prying eyes before passing a meal down into the cellar. She could feel it in the way her father's shoulders sagged at the end of the day, the unspoken worry that weighed him down. Every moment felt like walking on thin ice, the world beneath her feet fragile and ready to crack open with one misstep.

Maria's heart raced as Samuel spoke about freedom, the word sounding distant and foreign, as though it belonged to another world entirely. Her mind remained tethered to that cellar, to Sarah's hollow eyes watching her with a mix of gratitude and fear. Maria could still hear Sarah's breath, shallow and ragged in the dark, could still feel the oppressive dampness of the air in that hidden space. Each knock on the door at home sent a spike of panic through her, a fear that twisted itself deeper with every passing day. What would happen if the wrong person came to the door?

What would happen if the secret they held so carefully in their hands was exposed?

The weight of doing the right thing was heavier than Maria had ever imagined. It wasn't just a choice—it was a burden, one that settled across her shoulders like an invisible cloak, pulling her down with each step. She had done what was right, but the question that gnawed at her was whether she could keep doing it. Whether she could carry that fear, that terrible, all-consuming fear, and still move forward.

Maria shifted again in her seat, her grip on her dress tightening until her knuckles were white. She could feel the tension in the room as Samuel's words lingered in the air, but she was barely present. The word *freedom* floated before her, elusive, distant. She had done what was right, but at what cost? The weight of that question pressed down on her chest, heavier and heavier, until it felt like she might never be able to breathe freely again.

CHAPTER 7

Hans's Perspective

Hans leaned back in his chair, the worn wood creaking under his weight, and crossed his arms as the heated discussion about slavery filled the classroom. The voices of his classmates rose and fell in waves, but to Hans, they were little more than background noise. His mind drifted, tuning in and out of the debate, as his gaze wandered toward the window, the dull gray light of the city filtering in. He wasn't listening to Liam's fiery words or even to Samuel's measured tone—his thoughts were miles away, back in his father's study, where the world made sense.

He could almost hear his father's deep, resonant voice filling the room, the scent of cigars mixing with the crackle of the fireplace. His father's words always held a certain weight, carried a confidence that Hans had come to associate with truth itself. "New York's business depends on the South," his father would say, his voice calm but firm, as though explaining the simplest fact. "Cotton, sugar—without the Southern plantations, the entire economy would crumble. People don't like to talk about it, but that's the truth. It's all about keeping things in order."

Hans had grown up with these words, absorbing them as naturally as he breathed. They weren't just his father's opinions—

they were the foundation of his world. The Reinhardt & Sons Trading Company, built on the steady flow of Southern goods, had prospered on the backs of the very labor the classroom debate now condemned. Cheap, enslaved labor had made cotton and sugar flow north like rivers of gold, securing his family's fortune. For Hans, the idea of abolition wasn't just a moral issue bandied about in newspapers or classrooms—it was a direct threat to the life he had always known.

His gaze shifted to Liam, whose voice had risen in fervent defense of freedom and equality. The boy was practically vibrating with passion, his words tumbling out in an almost uncontrolled rush. To Hans, it was all so naïve. What did

Liam know about running a business, about the real pressures of keeping a family's legacy intact? The boy had come from Ireland with little more than the clothes on his back, and now he thought he could preach about freedom as if it were some magic cure-all. Liam's fiery ideals felt almost offensive in their simplicity, as if he didn't understand the complex, interconnected world that Hans had been raised in.

Hans's jaw tightened. Freedom. It was a fine enough idea, in theory, but it wasn't practical. Not in the real world. His father had always been a man of practicality, and Hans admired that about him. Practicality kept the company afloat, kept food on the table, and ensured that the Reinhardt name carried weight in the bustling economy of New York. Liam's idealism felt like a slap in the face to everything Hans had been taught, everything his father had worked to build.

He could hear his father's voice echoing in his mind, clear and authoritative: "You don't tear down a system without a plan for what comes after. Chaos is worse than order, no matter how unjust you think that order is."

The words pressed down on Hans like a weight. His family's wealth, their security, their place in the world—it was all built on that order, on a system that connected New York to the South through a web of trade and labor. The abolition of slavery wasn't just about freeing enslaved people—it was about dismantling the very foundation of the economy. And

without that foundation, Hans wondered, where would his family be? Where would New York be?

He glanced back at Liam, who was still speaking with the kind of passion that seemed untethered from reality. Liam's voice was filled with words like liberty, justice, and equality, lofty ideals that sounded good in a classroom but rang hollow to Hans. To Liam, freedom was a dream, an abstract ideal that could be achieved through speeches and protests. But to Hans, freedom was a threat, something that could unravel everything his family had built.

Hans's eyes narrowed. *Freedom isn't free,* he thought, his chest tightening with resentment. *It comes at a cost. And not everyone is willing to pay it.* His father had said as much in different ways over the years. Sacrifice was inevitable, but some sacrifices—like the collapse of an entire economy—were too great. The very idea of tearing apart the system without considering the consequences seemed reckless. The cost was too high.

He crossed his arms more tightly over his chest, feeling the weight of responsibility settle in his bones. This wasn't just about defending an abstract idea or winning an argument. Hans felt the burden of defending his family's way of life. He wasn't just sitting in a classroom, debating philosophical points with a boy who didn't understand the intricacies of trade and wealth. He was defending the legacy his father had built, the future he had been raised to protect.

Liam's impassioned speeches about freedom and equality might sway some of the other students, but not Hans. No amount of idealistic rhetoric was going to change the realities he had been taught since childhood. Practicality, order, and maintaining the delicate balance of the economy—those were the things that mattered. Without them, everything would fall apart, and no one—not even Liam—would be able to put it back together.

Hans shifted in his seat, the creak of the chair barely audible beneath the fervor of the debate. He wasn't moved by the passionate words or the calls for justice. His focus was clear: protect what's yours, preserve what's been built, and don't let anyone tear it down, even if they dress their ideals up in words like freedom.

Freedom, Hans thought bitterly, *isn't for everyone.*

CHAPTER 8

Liam's Irish Heritage

Liam clenched his fists under the desk, his knuckles white with tension as Hans's voice droned on, casually dismissing slavery as a "Southern issue." The indifferent tone in Hans's words made Liam's blood boil, his pulse quickening with anger that pulsed in his chest like a drumbeat. *Southern issue?* The phrase echoed in Liam's mind, each repetition igniting the sting of his own family's history. How could someone talk about slavery like it was just another business transaction? How could anyone be so blind?

His family had fled Ireland not so long ago, escaping British rule and the relentless grip of starvation. They'd left behind the land that had sustained their ancestors for generations, driven out by injustice. *"We left because we had no choice,"* his father had told him, his voice etched with the kind of pain that could never quite heal. *"They were starving us out, taking our crops, our land, our dignity. We came to America because it was supposed to be different. We came here to be free."* But now, sitting in this classroom in the so-called land of the free, Liam felt the bitter irony twist inside him like a knife. How could this country, this *beacon of freedom*, claim that title while it kept people in chains?

The memories of his father's stories came flooding back—

stories that had seeped into his bones as a child. Stories of hunger so deep it gnawed at your very soul, of entire villages hollowed out by famine. The Great Hunger, they called it. But Liam knew it wasn't just hunger—it was cruelty. It was the British landlords who exported crops while their own people starved to death in the streets. *"They treated us like animals,"* his father had said, his voice thick with both sorrow and a rage that time had not dulled.

Liam's jaw clenched as he remembered the tremor in his father's hands whenever he spoke of those dark days. The deep lines carved into his father's face were the kind of scars that no amount of distance from Ireland could erase. Since arriving in America, his father had worked the docks—hard, brutal work that bent his back and calloused his hands. But even after a day's toil, every night at dinner, his father would say, *"We came here for freedom, Liam. Don't ever forget that. We may be poor, but at least we're free."*

But sitting in this classroom, listening to Hans talk about laws and order like they were sacrosanct, that promise of freedom felt hollow to Liam. He had seen with his own eyes how laws could be used to oppress, to strip people of their humanity. His family had lived under laws that starved them, that turned them into beggars in their own homeland. Those laws had been called legal, but Liam knew better. They weren't laws—they were tools of oppression, designed to keep the powerful in power and the poor in chains.

Liam's fists slowly unclenched, but his heart still pounded in his chest as he leaned forward, his voice tight with restraint as he spoke. His eyes locked on Hans, sharp with anger that he barely kept in check. *"You talk about the law like it's something holy,"* Liam said, his words cutting through the classroom air. *"But not all laws are just. Some are meant to be broken. The laws in Ireland starved my family, drove us from our land. They called it legal, but it wasn't right.*" His voice cracked slightly under the weight of his own words, but he didn't flinch. He wouldn't let Hans's apathy silence him.

The room seemed to tighten around them, the air charged with the tension of the unspoken clash between two very different worlds. Liam could feel the weight of his father's words bearing down on him now, as if his family's struggle

was pressing down on his shoulders. His father had always told him that freedom wasn't something that was given—it was something you had to fight for, something you had to protect. *"You stand up for what's right, even if it costs you,"* his father would say, those words coming from a place of deep, hard-earned wisdom.

And now, in the heat of the classroom debate, Liam knew where he stood. He had seen what injustice looked like up close, and he wasn't going to sit quietly and watch it happen again, not in this country. Not now. Not ever.

Samuel's hands trembled ever so slightly as he unfolded the crinkled New York Times article he had purchased from Liam the day before. He stared at the bold headline: *Southern Slavery; A Glance at Uncle Tom's Cabin.* It was more than ink on paper—it was a spark, a fuse ready to ignite a nation already dry with tension. Holding the paper up for the class to see, Samuel's voice cut through the stillness of the room.

"This book," he began, his tone deliberate and steady, "is changing the way people think about slavery in this country." He let his words linger, watching the subtle shifts in posture, the flicker of discomfort that passed through his students. He knew this wasn't just a lesson—it was an invitation to confront the world as it was, not as they might wish it to be.

He glanced around the room, taking in the varied reactions on the faces of his students. Hans sat stiff in his seat, arms crossed tightly over his chest, his expression unreadable but tense. There was a cold resistance in his posture, the kind that spoke of entrenched ideas, passed down from generations who had much to lose. Liam, by contrast, looked ready to burst. His fists clenched so tightly his knuckles turned white, and his entire body leaned forward as if anticipating a fight that hadn't yet begun. Maria sat quietly, her gaze fixed on her lap, her hands clasped tightly together, trembling slightly, as though bracing for the weight of words she wasn't sure she was ready to hear.

"The South says it's exaggerated," Samuel continued, each word carefully measured. "The North sees it differently. But today, I'm not interested in what they say." He paused, feeling the growing tension in the room. "I want to know what you think."

The room was silent. It wasn't the usual classroom silence, filled with idle minds or the absence of noise. This was thick, charged—alive with thoughts unspoken. Samuel could feel it in the air, the conflict simmering just beneath the surface, the way each student was turning over the question in their mind, searching for the courage to speak.

Samuel turned back to the chalkboard where the word *freedom* still stood in stark, white letters. He tapped it lightly with his fingers. "Freedom," he said again, as if tasting the word. "It means something different to everyone. So, let's talk about what it means to you."

Hans shifted in his seat, the sound of wood creaking under his weight breaking the stillness. His eyes darted to Liam, as if anticipating the inevitable clash. Liam's body was taut, his face flushed with the force of his conviction, every muscle poised for a verbal onslaught.

Samuel decided to start with Hans. "Hans," he said, his tone even, "you've spoken before about the importance of order and structure. In your view, what does freedom mean in the context of this book? What does it mean for slavery?"

Hans hesitated. His eyes flickered with uncertainty, the rigid confidence he normally carried faltering under the pressure of the question. He uncrossed his arms but quickly folded them again, as though shielding himself from the vulnerability that came with answering. "Freedom..." he began, his voice cool but controlled, "it's important, sure. But it's not the only thing that matters. Order is what keeps society functioning. Without rules, without structure, freedom is just chaos."

He glanced at Liam, a silent challenge in his gaze. "Abolishing slavery might sound noble, but without a plan, it's just going to tear everything apart. The economy, people's livelihoods—there's more to think about than just ideals."

Liam shifted in his seat, his fists twitching. His voice came out sharp, almost trembling with restrained passion. "Freedom *is* the plan, Hans! You can't talk about rules when people are in chains, treated like animals. Rules don't matter when the system itself is wrong!" His voice rose, a raw edge of emotion breaking through. "You think the law is sacred? What about the laws that starved my family in Ireland? What about those? Laws don't make something right."

The room buzzed with the electricity of their exchange. Samuel could see the lines being drawn, not just between Hans and Liam, but in the hearts of every student watching. It wasn't just an argument—it was a reflection of the world they lived in, a world that was demanding answers to questions they barely knew how to ask.

Samuel intervened before the tension could spill over. "Liam," he said, gently but firmly, "freedom is powerful, but Hans raises an important point. What happens after? How do you build something new without tearing everything apart?"

Liam's eyes burned with intensity, but he remained silent, his jaw clenched. It was clear he wasn't backing down, but the weight of the question had given him pause. Samuel nodded, recognizing the struggle in Liam's silence. These were not easy questions.

Turning, Samuel's gaze settled on Maria, who had remained quiet throughout. Her eyes were still downcast, her fingers twisted together in her lap. "Maria," he said softly, "what does freedom mean to you?"

Her breath caught in her throat, and for a moment, Samuel thought she might not answer. But then, slowly, she lifted her gaze. Her voice, when it came, was soft, almost fragile, but there was strength beneath it. "Freedom..." she began, her words measured and deliberate, "freedom is being able to live without fear. To do what's right, even when it's hard." Her voice faltered slightly, but she continued, her tone gaining quiet resolve. "It's not just about what we want for ourselves. It's about doing what's right... even when it's dangerous."

The room fell into a deeper silence, Maria's words hanging in the air like a whispered truth that had been waiting to be spoken. Samuel saw the weight of her words settle on the faces of the students around her—on Hans, whose gaze flickered with something he wasn't ready to name, and on Liam, whose fists unclenched slightly, as if Maria's quiet courage had tempered his fiery passion.

In that moment, Samuel knew the lesson had begun, but it was far from over.

CHAPTER 9

Abigail's Role as a Future Teacher

As the classroom discussion swirled around *Uncle Tom's Cabin* and the heated debate on freedom, Samuel's attention drifted momentarily to the back of the room where Abigail sat, her posture straighter than usual, her hands folded neatly on her lap. For weeks, she had been an observer in his classroom—a quiet presence who seemed to absorb everything, yet remained cautious, uncertain of her place in this world of education. Today, though, Samuel sensed something different in her demeanor.

Abigail had always been a keen listener, her eyes wide with a curiosity that suggested she was more than just a passive participant in the lessons. She had the kind of quiet strength that made her easy to overlook at first, but Samuel had long recognized that beneath her calm exterior was a mind that was constantly at work, processing, questioning, and reflecting. Her silence wasn't disinterest—it was preparation.

Today, as the discussion about slavery and freedom intensified, Abigail's gaze wasn't wandering, as it sometimes did when the classroom noise grew too loud. Instead, her eyes were fixed on the conversation, her brow furrowed in thought. She wasn't just listening—she was weighing every word, every argument, with a discernment that was becoming more and more apparent.

Samuel caught her eye briefly, and in that fleeting moment, he saw something he hadn't noticed before—an eagerness, a hunger to participate. It wasn't the same fiery passion that fueled Liam's outbursts, nor the rigid pragmatism that anchored Hans's arguments. Abigail's expression was different. It was the look of someone who was searching, someone who was beginning to see her own role in these discussions, and perhaps, her role beyond them.

He made a mental note to speak with her after class.

Abigail had always been a bit of an enigma in the classroom, a student who excelled quietly but rarely spoke unless directly addressed. Her intelligence was evident, but she seemed to hold back, as if unsure whether her voice would carry the same weight as those around her. Yet, Samuel had seen glimpses of her potential—a thoughtful question here, a well-considered answer there—that hinted at something more. He wondered if she realized it yet, the potential she held within her to be a teacher herself.

As the debate raged on between Liam and Hans, Abigail shifted slightly in her seat. Her fingers toyed with the edge of her notebook, the pages worn from her meticulous note-taking. Samuel knew that she wasn't just absorbing the content of the lesson; she was studying him, watching the way he navigated the complex dynamics of the classroom, the way he guided discussions, and the way he allowed students to find their own voices. He suspected that she was imagining herself in his place, though she hadn't yet found the courage to admit it.

Abigail's path to teaching hadn't been planned. Like so many young women of her time, her future had once seemed predetermined—marriage, children, a life spent tending to a household. But something had shifted in her over the years, a restlessness that could no longer be ignored. Education, she had realized, was her way out. It was more than just a career—it was a calling, a way to shape the world beyond the narrow confines of domestic life.

Samuel had noticed her passion for learning early on. She devoured books in the way others devoured food, seeking knowledge like it was a necessity. It wasn't enough for her to know things—she wanted to understand them, to break them apart and see how they fit into the larger puzzle of the world. She was a natural teacher, though she hadn't yet embraced that part of herself.

When the bell rang, signaling the end of the lesson, Samuel watched as the students gathered their belongings, the energy from the debate still lingering in the air. Abigail moved with deliberate slowness, packing her books carefully, as if she was reluctant to leave the room. Samuel waited until the others had filed out before approaching her.

"Abigail," he said, his voice gentle but purposeful. "I've noticed something in you these past few weeks."

She looked up, her eyes widening slightly, but she said nothing. Her hands stilled, resting on the worn cover of her notebook.

"I've seen the way you listen, the way you observe," Samuel continued. "You have a gift for understanding more than just the surface of things. You think deeply, and I suspect you have much to say, even if you've been keeping it to yourself."

Abigail's cheeks flushed, and she dropped her gaze to the

floor. "I'm just... listening," she murmured, but there was a hesitancy in her voice, as if she wasn't entirely sure that was true anymore.

"Listening is important," Samuel agreed, "but there comes a time when listening isn't enough. You have insights that others in this class could benefit from. I can see it in the way you follow the discussions, the way you analyze what's being said. Have you ever thought about teaching?"

Abigail blinked, startled by the directness of the question. She had, of course, thought about it—more times than she could count. But the thought had always felt too big, too daunting, as if it belonged to someone else's life, not hers. She had admired Samuel's ability to guide his students, to ignite their minds, but she hadn't dared imagine herself in his position.

"I... I don't know," she stammered, her voice barely above a whisper. "I wouldn't know where to begin."

Samuel smiled, a warm, encouraging smile that softened the edges of her uncertainty. "None of us do at first. Teaching isn't something you just know how to do—it's something you learn. And from what I've seen, you're already on that path, even if you don't realize it yet."

Abigail bit her lip, the weight of his words settling over her. It was one thing to harbor the thought in the quiet corners of her mind, but to have someone else see it, to recognize it in her, was something entirely different. It made the possibility feel real.

"I've seen how you approach your studies," Samuel continued. "You're thorough, patient, and you care about getting it right. Those are qualities every good teacher needs. But more than that, you have a heart for it. You understand that education isn't just about facts—it's about helping others see the world in a new way."

Abigail looked up at him, her eyes searching his face for any sign that he might be exaggerating. But all she saw was sincerity, a belief in her that she hadn't yet found in herself.

"I'm not asking you to decide right now," Samuel said gently. "But I want you to think about it. I think you could be a remarkable teacher, Abigail. And when you're ready, I'll help you get there."

Abigail nodded slowly, her mind buzzing with the possibilities that Samuel had opened up for her. As she gathered her books and headed for the door, the weight of uncertainty still clung to her, but it was accompanied by something new—hope. For the first time, she could see a different future for herself, one where she wasn't just a student but a guide, helping others find their way through the complexities of the world.

And in that moment, as the door closed softly behind her, Abigail knew that this was only the beginning.

CHAPTER 10

Climax: Maria's Confession

The tension in the room was thick, almost unbearable, as the debate between Hans and Liam reached its boiling point. Hans sat rigid in his seat, his arms crossed tightly over his chest, while Liam leaned forward, his fists clenched, his knuckles white with anger. Samuel stood near the chalkboard, watching the two boys, sensing that the discussion was teetering on the edge of something explosive. Every student in the room seemed to hold their breath, caught in the crossfire of ideals.

"You don't understand!" Liam's voice cracked with raw emotion, his face flushed with frustration. "You talk about the law like it's some sacred thing, but not all laws are just! Some laws are meant to be broken—like the ones that starved my family in Ireland, the ones that let people die while the rich grew fat!"

Hans remained unmoved, his eyes narrowing as he regarded Liam's passionate outburst. "Your family's troubles don't compare," he said, his voice cold and dismissive. "The South is different. The law is the law, and people have to follow it. That's how order is maintained. You can't just pick and choose which laws to follow because they don't suit you." Liam's fists trembled at his sides, his voice rising. "So you'd send them back, then? If a runaway slave came to you, you'd hand them over like property?

You'd send them back to be beaten, to die, because that's what the law says?"

Hans's gaze hardened. "It's not our business, Liam. The law is clear. Slavery is legal in the South. If we start ignoring laws just because we don't like them, there's no order. There's only chaos."

Before Liam could respond, before Samuel could intervene, a soft but steady voice broke through the rising storm. The sound was unexpected, quiet at first, but it carried a weight that immediately drew everyone's attention.

Maria stood slowly from her seat near the window, her hands trembling as she clutched the edge of her desk. Her face was pale, her eyes wide and filled with a mix of fear and determination. Every head in the room turned toward her, the debate between Hans and Liam forgotten in an instant.

"I've been helping someone," Maria said, her voice barely above a whisper. But in the stillness of the classroom, her words echoed like thunder.

Samuel's breath caught in his throat. He had sensed something heavy weighing on Maria all day, but this—this was something else entirely.

Maria swallowed hard, her hands shaking visibly now as she continued. "A runaway slave. Her name is Sarah, and she's hiding nearby. "The room erupted into a stunned silence. No one moved. No one spoke. Even the dust motes hanging in the shafts of sunlight seemed to freeze in midair.

Liam's eyes widened, his anger forgotten in the face of Maria's revelation. Hans, for once, looked completely caught off guard, his cold, calculated expression faltering as he stared at Maria in disbelief.

Samuel felt his heart lurch in his chest. He had known that

Maria carried something deep inside her, something unspoken, but he hadn't expected this. He could see the fear in her eyes, the way her entire body trembled with the weight of her confession. Yet, there was a strength in her voice—a strength that came from knowing the stakes, from living in a world where the right thing wasn't always the easy thing.

"I've been bringing her food," Maria said, her voice growing stronger, though her hands still shook. "She's been hiding in the cellar of our home for weeks. I've tried to keep her safe, but... every day, I'm afraid someone will find out. I'm afraid... I'm afraid of what will happen to her. To us."

Her words hung in the air, raw and exposed, cutting through the arguments about law and order, about freedom and justice. This wasn't a theoretical debate anymore. This was real. This was life and death.

Hans was the first to speak, though his voice was quieter now, less sure than before. "You're... you're breaking the law, Maria. You could be arrested. Your family could lose everything. You're risking... everything."

Maria met his gaze, her eyes fierce despite the tremor in her voice. "I know. And I don't care. The law doesn't matter when it's wrong. Sarah deserves her freedom. She deserves to live. And I won't stand by and let the law tell me otherwise."

Liam's chest swelled with something like admiration, his anger replaced by awe at Maria's courage. "You're doing what's right, Maria," he said softly. "No matter what Hans says, no matter what the law says—what you're doing is right."

Hans looked away, his jaw clenched, his mind clearly grappling with Maria's words. For the first time, he seemed uncertain, as if the rigid world of rules and order that he had always relied on was beginning to crack at the edges.

Samuel stepped forward, his voice calm but filled with gravity. "Maria," he said gently, "what you've done... it's incredibly brave. But it's also dangerous. Helping a runaway slave... it's a risk not just for you, but for your family."

Maria nodded, her eyes brimming with tears. "I know. But I couldn't just turn her away. I couldn't live with myself if I did nothing."

Samuel's heart ached with the weight of the moment, with the knowledge that this young girl, sitting in his classroom,

Had taken on a burden far heavier than any child should have to carry. And yet, she had made her choice. She had chosen to act, to stand against the injustice she saw, even when it meant risking everything.

In that moment, Samuel knew that this was the true lesson of the day—not the words written on the chalkboard or the debates over law and freedom. It was Maria's quiet courage, her willingness to act despite her fear that would leave the lasting impact on everyone in that room.

And as he looked around at the faces of his students—Liam, filled with fiery determination; Hans, struggling with the weight of his own beliefs; and Maria, standing tall in her vulnerability—Samuel realized that this classroom, this moment, was where change began.

As Maria's trembling words filled the room, Samuel felt a deep, unmistakable shift in the atmosphere. The debates about slavery and freedom, which had been abstract and theoretical just moments before, were now brutally real. Maria's confession hit him like a blow to the chest—raw, heavy, and undeniably human.

For a moment, Samuel stood frozen, the weight of the revelation pressing down on him. He had come to this city with grand ideals, a belief that education could shape young minds, prepare them to grapple with the world's harshest realities. But now, faced with this brave young girl who had put herself and her family at grave risk, he realized the enormity of his task. This wasn't just about teaching—it was

About navigating the messy, dangerous waters of morality in a deeply unjust world.

He could feel his heart pounding in his chest. He was responsible for these children, for their safety, for their education—but how could he reconcile that with the fact that one of them had chosen to defy the law, to risk her life for someone else's freedom? And more than that, how could he respond in a way that honored Maria's bravery while protecting her?

Samuel inhaled deeply, steadying himself. His eyes met Maria's, and in that instant, he saw everything she was carrying—fear, resolve, and the quiet strength of someone who had already accepted the cost of doing the right thing.

He stepped forward, his voice soft but filled with conviction. "Maria," he said, "What you've done is incredibly brave. You've shown more courage than most adults I know. But you must understand, the risks you've taken—they're real. They're dangerous."

Maria's eyes didn't waver, though her hands still trembled at her sides. "I know," she whispered, her voice strained but resolute. "But I couldn't just turn her away. I couldn't."

Samuel felt the words catch in his throat. He wanted to tell her she was right, that what she had done was just, noble, necessary. But he also knew the dark reality of the world outside this classroom. The Fugitive Slave Act of 1850 was a looming threat, one that made it illegal for anyone to harbor or assist an escaped slave. People were being arrested, fined, and even imprisoned for doing exactly what Maria had done.

He glanced at the other students, seeing the mix of emotions on their faces—shock, admiration, fear. This was no longer a debate about distant concepts of law and justice; this was about life and death, about people they might know, and the terrifying consequences of stepping outside the law.

Samuel knew he had to tread carefully. He couldn't condone breaking the law outright—not here, not now, with the children watching. But neither could he stand by and let Maria believe that her actions were anything less than heroic.

His voice dropped, low and serious. "You've done something incredibly selfless," he said, looking into her eyes, making sure she felt the weight of his words. "But Maria, the world is not kind to people who do what's right when it goes against the law. You need to be careful—very careful."

He paused, letting the gravity of the situation sink in, not just for Maria, but for the entire class. "There are some things," he continued slowly, "that are bigger than the law. There are some moments when doing what's right means taking risks—risks that could cost us everything. But we have to be smart. We have to think about the consequences, not just for ourselves, but for the people we're trying to protect."

Samuel's heart ached as he spoke, the conflict of teacher, protector, and moral guide pulling him in different directions. He didn't want to snuff out Maria's courage, but he also knew he had a responsibility to ensure she understood the full scope of the danger she was in.

The room was still, every student hanging on his words, waiting to see where he would go next. Samuel straightened slightly, his voice gaining strength as he addressed the class as a whole. "This is the world we live in," he said. "We are confronted with choices every day—some that feel impossible, some that test the very core of who we are. What Maria has done is brave, and it's right. But it also reminds us that sometimes, doing what's right is the hardest thing we can do."

He paused, glancing from Liam, whose face was filled with admiration for Maria, to Hans, who was still wrestling with the enormity of what had just been revealed. "There are laws," Samuel said, his voice firm, "and there is justice. And sometimes, those two things are not the same."

He let that hang in the air for a moment, knowing that the lesson they were learning today went far beyond the classroom walls.

Then, turning back to Maria, his expression softened. "You've taken a risk that most people would never dream of taking," he said. "And you've shown a strength and compassion that we all should strive for. But you're not alone in this. We'll find a way to make sure that you, your family, and Sarah are safe."

For the first time, Maria's tough exterior cracked, her eyes glistening with unshed tears as she nodded, relieved and yet still scared.

Samuel felt the full weight of his role settle over him—not just as a teacher, but as someone responsible for guiding these children through a world filled with moral grayness, a world where laws didn't always align with what was right.

The moment had passed, but the room was still charged with the gravity of what had been said. And in that silence, Samuel knew that this was one of the most important lessons they would ever learn—not from books or lectures, but from the courage of one young girl, who had chosen to risk everything for what she believed was right.

CHAPTER 11

Samuel's Evolution and Resolution

Samuel felt his heart swell with both pride and fear as the weight of the moment settled over him. This was the moment he had been waiting for—the moment when his students would confront the realities of the world beyond the classroom. But it was more than that. It was also the moment when Samuel realized how deeply intertwined his role as a teacher was with the broader moral and social currents swirling around them all.

He had arrived in New York with the simple ambition of teaching children arithmetic and reading, believing that knowledge alone could equip them for life. But as he stood in the hushed classroom, his eyes scanning the faces of his students—Liam's fiery passion, Hans's conflicted defiance, Maria's quiet courage—he understood that the lessons they truly needed went far beyond the textbooks. These children weren't just learning facts and figures; they were learning how to navigate the complex moral landscape of a world filled with injustice, conflict, and uncertainty.

Samuel thought of **Frederick Douglass's** words once more,

echoing in his mind: *"It is easier to build strong children than to repair broken men."* Douglass's insight had always inspired Samuel, but now, in this small, dim classroom, it resonated in a new way. Building strong children wasn't just about teaching them skills for a profession. It was about equipping them with the strength of character to question the world around them, to stand up for what was right even when it was difficult or dangerous.

As he looked at Maria, still trembling from her confession about Sarah, the runaway slave she had helped, Samuel realized that his role wasn't to shield these children from the harsh truths of the world. It was to guide them through it. In many ways, Maria had already shown more bravery than most adults he knew. She had made a choice that would forever change her view of herself and the world around her. The weight of her decision was clear on her young face, but there was also a quiet strength that told Samuel she wouldn't turn back.

Hans, too, had begun to evolve. His rigid belief in law and order had cracked under the pressure of Maria's confession. For the first time, Samuel saw uncertainty in the boy's eyes—a sign that the unyielding truths passed down from his father no longer seemed so absolute. Hans had grown up believing that the world operated on clear rules and structures, but Samuel could see him grappling with the understanding that those rules weren't always just. Perhaps, over time, Hans would learn to balance his pragmatic instincts with a deeper sense of empathy and justice.

And then there was Liam. The boy's unrelenting passion for freedom and equality had been born from his family's struggle as Irish immigrants, but now, he was beginning to see that freedom wasn't just a slogan to be shouted—it was a complex, nuanced idea that required careful thought and consideration. Liam had the fire of a revolutionary, but Samuel knew that his greatest challenge would be learning patience—understanding that true change took time and strategy, not just raw emotion.

For Samuel, this was a moment of transformation. He had come to the city to teach, but now he realized that teaching was far more than filling young minds with information. It was about guiding them through the moral dilemmas they would face, helping them understand that sometimes doing the right thing wasn't easy or clear. It meant giving them the tools to think critically, to question, to debate, and to stand up for what they believed in, even when the world pushed back.

The classroom felt different now. It wasn't just a place for rote learning; it was a space where ideas collided, where different worldviews were tested and refined. Samuel understood that his role was to create an environment where these collisions could happen, safely and constructively. The chalkboard behind him, smeared with the remnants of their lesson on freedom, seemed to take on new meaning. The word "freedom" wasn't just a topic for discussion—it was a living, breathing concept that these children were beginning to grasp, each in their own way.

As the students began to gather their belongings and leave, the tension of the day slowly dissolving into the routine of the afternoon, Samuel remained standing at the front of the classroom, lost in thought. Tomorrow, they would face new challenges, new lessons. But today, something important had shifted. They had all, in some way, taken a step toward understanding the complexity of the world.

Samuel exhaled slowly, the weight of his own journey settling on his shoulders. He wasn't just shaping the minds of the next generation—he was shaping the future. His students, with their different backgrounds and perspectives, were a reflection of the city itself: vibrant, diverse, and brimming with potential. In the quiet

aftermath of the day's lesson, he realized that if he could guide them through these moral and ethical challenges, he wasn't just teaching them to survive in the world—they would have the power to change it.

He walked slowly to the window, gazing out at the bustling streets below. The noise of the city was muffled through the glass, but he could still see the throngs of people moving through the streets—immigrants, workers, mothers, children. The future of New York, and perhaps even the country, was unfolding right there before him. Samuel smiled softly to himself, knowing that, in some small way, he and his students were part of that future.

The bell rang, signaling the end of the day, and Samuel turned back to the emptying classroom. Tomorrow would bring new challenges, but for the first time, Samuel felt a deep sense of purpose. He had not only found his place as a teacher—he had found his role as a mentor, a guide, and a force for change.

CHAPTER 12

Transition to the Next Story:

As Samuel tidied up the chalkboard, the remnants of their lesson still visible in the dust, he noticed Abigail lingering by the doorway, her books clutched tightly in her arms. There was something in her expression—a quiet determination that Samuel hadn't seen before. He nodded to her, and she returned the gesture with a small, knowing smile.

It would be some time before Samuel understood the full impact he had made on Abigail, but in that moment, he sensed that a new chapter was beginning—not just for her, but for all of them. Tomorrow, they would continue their journey together, with new lessons, new questions, and new opportunities to grow.

And as Abigail stepped into the hallway, the seeds of her own future—one that Samuel would one day witness with pride—had already begun to take root.

End of Story

Afterword

The Mentor's Chalk is the first story in *The Old is Forever New* series, a collection that explores critical moments in American history through the lens of education and moral evolution. Set in New York City in 1853, this story aims to capture the complexities of a rapidly changing society on the brink of civil unrest. As immigration swelled, the urban landscape transformed, and debates over slavery intensified, education became a key battleground for ideas that would shape the nation's future.

The character of Samuel represents the ideals of a teacher striving to navigate these turbulent times while imparting wisdom and critical thinking to his students. His journey through the city, and ultimately his classroom, is a reflection of the larger societal struggles—where poverty, injustice, and the fight for freedom converge.

In writing this story, I drew from primary historical sources, including articles from *The New York Times* and the speeches of Frederick Douglass, to root the narrative in authenticity. Samuel's classroom discussion on *Uncle Tom's Cabin* reflects the real national debates that were happening at the time. By bringing characters like Maria, Liam, and Hans into this mix, I hoped to show the varying perspectives of people—immigrants, privileged families, and those living in fear—who were navigating the same moral dilemmas but from different vantage points.

At its core, *The Mentor's Chalk* is about the power of education to challenge assumptions, change minds, and inspire courageous action. Samuel's evolution, from a teacher uncertain of his role to one who embraces his duty to guide young minds through moral complexity, is central to the story's message. His interactions with students like Maria, who risk everything to help a runaway slave, and Abigail, who quietly emerges as a future leader, are meant to reflect the true stakes of education.

While the story is fictional, it is grounded in the real history of New York City, the abolitionist movement, and the moral conflicts of the time. The journey Samuel embarks on is just the beginning. As the series continues, these characters will grow, and the next generation will face new challenges, continuing the cycle of mentorship and moral awakening.

It is my hope that readers will find themselves reflecting on the same questions Samuel poses to his students: What does freedom mean? How do we balance order and justice? And perhaps most importantly, how do we find the courage to act when the world asks us to?

Thank you for joining me on this journey, and I hope you continue with us through the rest of The Old is Forever New series.

References & Sources for Historical Context:

Frederick Douglass' Writings and Speeches:

Douglass, Frederick. *Narrative of the Life of Frederick Douglass, an American Slave.* 1845.

Douglass, Frederick. *What to the Slave Is the Fourth of July?* Speech, July 5, 1852.

Douglass' views on education as the "pathway from slavery to freedom" were central to the portrayal of Samuel's motivations.

The Public School Society of New York:

Snyder, Edwin D. *The Public School Society of New York: Its History, Condition, and Prospects.* New York, 1853.

Information on the Society's role in expanding education in the mid-19th century and its contribution to shaping the landscape of public schooling in New York City during this period.

New York City Construction in 1853:

Burrows, Edwin G., and Mike Wallace. *Gotham: A History of New York City to 1898.* Oxford University Press, 1999.

This book provided details about the rapid urbanization and construction boom in mid-19th-century New York City.

Insight into the development of infrastructure, including brownstone buildings and tenement housing.

Slavery and Abolition in New York City:

Harris, Leslie M. *In the Shadow of Slavery: African Americans in New York City, 1626-1863*. University of Chicago Press, 2003.

An examination of the complex relationship between slavery, abolitionism, and urban life in New York City, particularly through the lens of debates surrounding *Uncle Tom's Cabin*.

The discussion of the impact of Harriet Beecher Stowe's novel on both the North and South was drawn from this work.

Street Life and Immigrant Communities in 1850s New York:

Anbinder, Tyler. *Five Points: The 19th-Century New York City Neighborhood That Invented Tap Dance, Stole Elections, and Became the World's Most Notorious Slum*. Free Press, 2001.

Provides a detailed description of life in lower Manhattan's immigrant neighborhoods, focusing on the Irish and Italian communities, which influenced the setting and characters like Liam, the paperboy.

New York Times Archives:

New York Daily Times (renamed *The New York Times*). 1853 articles discussing urban life, Irish immigration, and Southern slavery. Specific reference: *Southern Slavery: A Glance at Uncle Tom's Cabin*, which was a real article from the period that captured the national debate around slavery.

Reference List for *The Mentor's Chalk*

Frederick Douglass' Writings and Speeches

Douglass, Frederick. *Narrative of the Life of Frederick Douglass, an American Slave.* 1845.

Douglass, Frederick. *What to the Slave Is the Fourth of July?* Speech, July 5, 1852.

Douglass' views on education as the "pathway from slavery to freedom" provided key thematic elements in Samuel's motivations.

The Public School Society of New York

Snyder, Edwin D. *The Public School Society of New York: Its History, Condition, and Prospects.* New York, 1853.

Details about the role of the Public School Society in expanding education in New York City and shaping the landscape of public schooling, adding context to Samuel's teaching mission.

New York City Construction in 1853

Burrows, Edwin G., and Mike Wallace. *Gotham: A History of New York City to 1898.* Oxford University Press, 1999.

This source provides details about the rapid urbanization and construction in New York, including brownstones and tenement housing, which are central to the setting in *The Mentor's Chalk.*

The Hotel Saint Nicholas (1853)

Anbinder, Tyler. *Five Points: The 19th-Century New York City*

Neighborhood That Invented Tap Dance, Stole Elections, and Became the World's Most Notorious Slum. Free Press, 2001.

The contrast between the luxurious **Hotel Saint Nicholas** and the more humble boarding house where Samuel stays highlights the class differences in 1850s New York. This source covers the broader context of economic disparities and hospitality in the city.

Slavery and Abolition in New York City

Harris, Leslie M. *In the Shadow of Slavery: African Americans in New York City, 1626-1863.* University of Chicago Press, 2003.

Provides context on slavery and abolitionism in New York, including reactions to *Uncle Tom's Cabin,* which is central to the classroom discussions in the story.

Street Life and Immigrant Communities in 1850s New York

Anbinder, Tyler. *Five Points: The 19th-Century New York City Neighborhood That Invented Tap Dance, Stole Elections, and Became the World's Most Notorious Slum.* Free Press, 2001.

Describes immigrant life in New York, focusing on the Irish, Italian, and German communities, which influenced the creation of characters like Liam, the Irish paperboy, and the boarding house setting.

New York Times Archives

New York Daily Times (now *The New York Times*). Various articles from 1853.

Specific references to real articles, including *Southern Slavery;*

A Glance at Uncle Tom's Cabin, which was published during this period and reflects the national debate on slavery.

Harriet Beecher Stowe's Uncle Tom's Cabin

Stowe, Harriet Beecher. *Uncle Tom's Cabin; or, Life Among the Lowly.* 1852.

This novel sparked national conversations about slavery and was central to the historical and moral debates depicted in the classroom.

www.ingramcontent.com/pod-product-compliance
Lightning Source LLC
Chambersburg PA
CBHW040840010826
48978CB00012BB/841